Best Friends

Written by Bonnie Brooke

He's jazzy, she's classy.
He's cool and she's sweet.
But best friends can dance
To the same snappy beat.

These two friends are true friends.
"Miss Lady!" they say.
"You've got a new collar!
Well, it's a fine day!"

Let's jump and let's romp!
Come frolic and run!
For true friends want new friends
To join in the fun!

Hello! Who are you?
And where have you been?
I'll show you around,
And you'll fit right in!

A muzzle's no puzzle
When best friends help out.
And now Lady's free
To go romping about!

How high we can fly!
What dreams we can dare!
When best friends team up,
They can soar anywhere!

True hearts are two hearts
That love one another.
And best friends are sometimes
A father and mother.

The day says, "Let's play!"
The world says, "I'm yours!"
Adventures await
In the big, bright outdoors.

Caring and sharing,
At playtime and rest.
Sweet friends like you
Are the best of the best!

The End